As they got closer, the Aldens could hear their friend Katharine calling out. "I think something bit me!" she said, flailing about in the water.

"Swim to the boat," her grandfather called back.

But Katharine didn't seem to be listening, so her grandfather went to the edge of the boat and started to climb over.

"We can help her," Jessie called to him as their own boat approached.

"Jessie, wait!" said Benny. "You don't know what could be out there."

Jessie scanned the shallow water. "There's nothing here, Benny. Don't let those old stories of sea monsters worry you. Everything will be okay."

Benny wasn't so sure. But before he could say another word, Jessie and Henry jumped into the water and started swimming toward their friend.

THE BOXCAR CHILDREN®

CREATED BY
GERTRUDE CHANDLER WARNER

CREATURES OF LEGEND

BOOK 3

MERMAIDS OF THE DEEP BLUE SEA

STORY BY DEE GARRETSON

ALBERT WHITMAN & COMPANY
CHICAGO, ILLINOIS

Copyright © 2021 by Albert Whitman & Company
First published in the United States of America
in 2021 by Albert Whitman & Company

ISBN 978-0-8075-0806-0 (hardcover)
ISBN 978-0-8075-0816-9 (paperback)
ISBN 978-0-8075-0818-3 (ebook)

THE BOXCAR CHILDREN® is a registered trademark
of Albert Whitman & Company.

Printed in the United States of America
10 9 8 7 6 5 4 3 2 1 LB 26 25 24 23 22 21

Illustrations by Thomas Girard

Visit The Boxcar Children® online at www.boxcarchildren.com.
For more information about Albert Whitman & Company,
visit our website at www.albertwhitman.com.

CONTENTS

CHAPTER 1

THE HOUSE ON THE HILL

What brings you to Puerto Rico?" the flight attendant asked fourteen-year-old Henry Alden. "Are you visiting family?"

Henry's little brother, Benny, was following him up the aisle of the airplane. "We're searching for sea monsters!" he said.

The flight attendant chuckled. "Is that so?" she asked.

"We really are!" said Benny. He held up a toy

shark and a toy alligator and pretended they were chasing each other.

"It's kind of a long story," Henry explained. "We're visiting a friend of our grandfather."

"Well, this works out perfectly," the flight attendant said. She stopped at a row where a young girl was sitting. The girl's hair was tied in purple ribbons, and she had a purple stuffed animal on her lap. "This is Katharine. She's visiting family too. And she's ten, just like you, Violet. We've arranged to seat you all together for the flight."

"Hi," said Violet. "I like your outfit. Purple is my favorite color." Violet turned to Jessie, who was twelve. "I'll give up my turn to sit by the window and sit by Katharine instead. Benny, you can have the window seat."

"Yay!" Benny cheered. "Maybe I'll spot a shipwreck or a giant sea monster!"

Before long the plane was in the air, and Katharine turned to Violet. "Is it true what your brother said? Are you really going to look for sea monsters?"

"Benny can be a little bit…dramatic," Violet said.

She looked over at her six-year-old brother. He had taken out a plastic octopus and was making sound effects with his cheeks as it swam through the air.

"We're helping our grandfather's friend," Violet said. "She's doing a television show for kids. It's about legendary creatures. We're helping her investigate."

"Wow, that sounds amazing," said Katharine. "What kinds of legendary creatures?"

Benny leaned around Violet. "First, we learned about bigfoots in Colorado. Then, in Iceland, we looked for elves and trolls. Now—sea monsters!"

"We don't know exactly what we'll be looking for at this stop," said Violet. "Just that it has to do with the water."

"Does your grandfather live in Puerto Rico?" Jessie asked Katharine.

"No, but he's writing a book that takes place there. He rented a big boat, and we're going to stay on it while he does research."

"You get to sleep on a boat?" Benny asked. "I hope we can do that."

Henry spoke up from across the aisle. "What kind of books does your grandfather write?"

"Exciting ones!" Katharine answered. "Except they're for grown-ups, so I haven't read them. Are you going to learn about luscas too? My grandfather is putting one of those in his book."

"What's that?" Benny asked.

Katharine shuddered. "They are terrible sea monsters that come up out of the water and wrap their tentacles around you." She hugged her stuffed animal close.

Benny's eyes grew wider. "Really?"

Katharine nodded. "Some of them are so big their tentacles can wrap around boats and sink them. I wish I had some paper. I could draw you a picture."

Violet took out a notepad and a pencil case and handed them to Katharine.

"I've heard of the lusca before," Henry said. "It's another legendary creature, Benny."

"Luscas aren't just a legend," Katharine said as she started to draw. "I've read about them on the Internet." The girl drew a creature that had a shark's head and a body like an octopus with too many tentacles. "There are lots of websites about it."

"Some things on the Internet aren't true," said Jessie.

"You check them out. You'll see." Katharine added in some sharp teeth to the creature's mouth. She held up the drawing. "Isn't it scary?"

Benny looked at Katharine's picture. He didn't mind sharks and octopuses, but he didn't like the thought of both of them together. "Maybe I don't want to stay on a boat after all," he said. "I hope that's not what we're looking for."

"I don't like them either," Violet said. "But it's a good drawing. Do you want to draw mermaids with me? That's one legendary creature I want to learn more about."

"Sure," Katharine said. "I'm better at drawing manatees though." She held up her stuffed animal.

5

"This is Winston. I draw him all the time."

Violet noticed Winston had a polka-dot tail. "Do real manatees have polka dots on them?" she asked.

Katharine giggled. "No. A friend made Winston for me. Real manatees aren't purple either. They're gray. But I wanted to see what a purple manatee with a polka-dot tail would look like." Then Katharine got a little shy. "I know it's silly, but I like it."

Violet smiled. "I like it too."

Violet and Katharine talked and drew for the rest of the trip. Henry and Jessie read. And Benny went back to playing with his sea animals. Before long the plane wheels touched down, and everyone on the flight began to cheer and clap.

Benny clapped along. Then he looked up at Jessie. "What's going on?"

A woman in the next row turned around and smiled. "It's a tradition for people from Puerto Rico," she explained. "We always cheer when we return. We're happy to be home."

"I like that tradition," said Benny.

The Alden children got off the plane with Katharine, and an airline employee brought them to pick up their bags.

"Don't we have to go through customs?" Violet asked. "We had to do that when we visited Iceland."

"No," Henry said. "Puerto Rico is part of the United States."

"I never knew this was a state!" said Benny.

Jessie shook her head. "Puerto Rico is a territory, not a state. But all of the people here are American citizens."

"That's right," the airline employee said. "Many younger visitors don't know that. I'm glad you do."

Jessie nodded. She liked to be prepared for their adventures. "I read that this airport is pretty small. We should be able to find Dr. Iris in no time."

"I can't wait to see my grandfather," Katharine said. She peered around the people passing by. "There he is!"

A bald man in a bright, flowery shirt waved at her, and she ran toward him. Then Katharine took him

7

by the hand and pulled him over to the Aldens.

"These are my new friends from the plane," Katharine explained. She introduced them.

Katharine's grandfather greeted the Aldens with a smile. "Nice to meet you," he said. "I'm sorry we can't stay and chat. We have lots of exciting adventures planned."

"We heard you were going to look for a lusca," said Jessie. "Is that true?"

"Luscas aren't the only interesting things I'll be looking for," he said. "Just since I've arrived, I've heard stories of even more interesting things in the deep sea. Now let's go find your bag, Katharine."

"Okay. Bye, Aldens," the girl said as she followed him.

"Bye! Watch out for sea monsters!" Benny called.

Violet was sad to see her new friend go. "I wonder if we'll see her again."

Jessie shrugged. "You never know. It sounds like her grandfather is interested in just the types of things we'll be looking for with Dr. Iris."

The Aldens grabbed their bags and went with the attendant. While they waited for Dr. Iris, Violet noticed a bright advertisement. "It's a sign for a mermaid tour!" she said.

The sign had a picture of a pretty mermaid with a sparkly green-and-silver tail.

"Mermaid tour, huh?" said Henry. "I wonder if that's the creature we'll be looking for."

Benny tipped his head to the side. "Why would we look for it? There's one right there."

Jessie laughed. "I think that's a picture of someone dressed up as a mermaid, Benny," she said. "We're here for the real thing."

"That's right," said Henry. "Remember, we need to find evidence if we are going to say that something is real."

"Did I hear my favorite word?" said a woman with short gray hair.

"Dr. Iris!" Benny gave her a hug. Then he pulled away. "Is *mermaid* your favorite word?"

"*Evidence* is my favorite word," Dr. Iris said. She

gave a little smile. "But *mermaid* is a good one too."

"Is that what we are going to be learning about?" Violet asked.

"It sounds like you children have solved one mystery already," said Dr. Iris, nodding. She signed a piece of paper from the airline employee, and they made their way out of the airport.

"Where are we going first?" Henry asked. He couldn't imagine what the first step in studying mermaids would be.

"Are we going out to sea?" Benny asked.

"Not just yet," said Dr. Iris. "First we're going home."

Benny stopped walking. "Home? But we just got here!"

Violet leaned over to her brother. "I don't think she means our home, Benny."

It didn't take long to reach their first stop. Dr. Iris turned her car up a narrow road, and a big house at the top of a hill came into view. It was made of white stone blocks and had three levels, each with

11

big windows and balconies that wrapped around the building.

"It's so…round," said Benny.

"That is because this house was designed to withstand hurricanes," said Dr. Iris. She pointed up to the circular-shaped house. "When the wind hits the walls, it flows around the building."

"Wow," said Violet. "That's very smart."

"The weather and the sea affect a lot of things on this island," said Dr. Iris. She added, "From the shapes of the buildings to the stories people tell."

When the group got closer, they could see the bottom level was a parking area. "The garage was built to be partway open so the winds can blow underneath the house and through this level."

"Dr. Iris, you know a lot about this place," said Violet. "Do you know the person who lives here?"

Dr. Iris gave a small smile. "Yes, but it has been some time since I have visited."

"Is that an elevator?" Henry asked, pointing to a metal door.

Dr. Iris nodded. "Should we take the elevator or the stairs?"

"Elevator!" Benny cried. "Do you think Grandfather would put an elevator in our house?" he asked Jessie. "I like to push the buttons."

Jessie laughed. "I don't think so, but it would be fun."

"I got a text message that says we are to go on in," Dr. Iris said, punching a code into a keypad on the elevator. "Something has come up, but the person we're meeting will be back as soon as she can. Gina, her assistant, will meet us."

When the elevator dinged, the door opened to a large room. Bookshelves filled the center of the room. Beyond those were tables and chairs next to windows that looked out over the ocean on one side and the mountains on the other. Framed maps hung on the walls between the windows, and a large desk and chair sat near the elevator.

"This is the library," Dr. Iris said. "It is one of the largest collections of books on legendary creatures in the world. Scholars and artists from all over come to visit."

"Wow," said Violet, walking up to one of the shelves. "Whoever lives here must be very important."

Everything was so neat; Violet was afraid to touch any of the books. Then Dr. Iris picked one out and handed it to her.

"I think you might find this one particularly interesting," she said.

The book had a picture of a creature with a lion's head and an eagle's body on the cover. Inside, Violet noticed handwritten words on the first page: *For Iris. From your tía.*

"Dr. Iris, this book has your name in it," said Violet. "Does that mean it's yours?"

Dr. Iris smiled. "You children don't miss much, do you? I was going to wait until my tía got here to tell you, but I guess the secret is out. This house belongs to my aunt. Growing up, it was like my second home."

"This was *your* house?" asked Violet. She knew

that Dr. Iris was smart. As a paleontologist, it seemed like she knew all there was to know about every animal that had ever existed. She also seemed to know all about creatures that *might* exist. Now Violet could see why.

Benny looked confused. "If this is your home," he said, "why didn't you clap and cheer when we got here?"

Jessie explained about the people returning to Puerto Rico on the airplane.

Dr. Iris chuckled. "I will have to do that in the future, Benny," she said. "Just not when I am the one driving the car!"

The children roamed the library, looking at books and admiring maps. Some of the creatures in the books looked scary. But somehow, knowing Dr. Iris had grown up in the library made it less scary.

The elevator dinged, and a woman hobbled out with a cane. She looked very much like Dr. Iris, except her hair was white instead of gray. The two greeted with a big hug.

"This is my aunt, Professor Marcela Reyes," said Dr. Iris.

"Call me Tía Chela," the woman said. "Everyone in my family does. I've heard so much about you that I think of you as my family too."

She turned back to Dr. Iris. "I am sorry I was not here when you arrived." The woman's smile faded.

"What is it?" asked Dr. Iris. "Is something wrong?"

Tía Chela sighed. "It's a friend of mine. You know him, Iris—Antonio Amador, the ecologist who lives out on the island?"

"Yes, of course," said Dr. Iris. "Has something happened?"

Tía Chela nodded slowly. "I think he might be missing."

LEGENDS AROUND THE WORLD

"Antonio hasn't been heard from in two weeks," Tía Chela said. "The last boat to leave him supplies just dropped them off at the dock on his island. Antonio wasn't there to receive them like he usually is."

Tía Chela sat down in a chair. She winced as she straightened her leg. "He's my age. He shouldn't live alone, but he won't listen when I tell him that. He's never listened. I've just finished arranging for a boat to take me out to check on him."

"That is worrisome," Dr. Iris said. "I remember Antonio from when I was little. The other children were scared of him, but I loved listening to the stories he told. He talked about animals like they were friends of his. People joked that he liked creatures of the sea more than he liked creatures of the land— humans. His nickname is Doc Pez." She turned to the children. "*Pez* means 'fish' in Spanish."

"Doctor Fish," said Benny. "That's a funny nickname."

"It is," Tía Chela agreed. "But he likes it. And yes, he's happy being alone on his island. He's always thinking of ways to keep boats from bringing people there, but he's never been out of contact for this long."

"You shouldn't go out on a boat until your leg is feeling better," Dr. Iris said. "Why don't the children and I go? Doc Pez was one of the first people I wanted to talk to about our investigation."

Tía Chela seemed unsure. "The island is quite far by boat. Are you children up to it?"

"Yes!" Henry said. The others agreed just as readily.

Tía Chela smiled. "I admit, I'm relieved I don't have to make the trip. I'll have to introduce you to Gina, my assistant. She was one of Doc Pez's students. She's the one who told me he was missing. Have you seen her?"

Dr. Iris shook her head. "There was no one here when we arrived."

"Will one of you check the main desk and see if there is a note on it?" Tía Chela asked.

Jessie went over to a desk by the elevator, but there was no note.

"Strange," Tía Chela said. "It's not like her not to let me know where she's going. I hope she returns soon. The last thing I need is two missing people!"

A buzzer sounded. It was coming from an intercom. "Maybe that's her," said Violet.

Dr. Iris went to the intercom and pressed a button.

The voice on the other end was a man's. "Delivery for Professor Reyes," the voice said.

"Yes, come up the elevator to the second floor," Dr. Iris replied. She punched in a code, and soon the elevator door opened. A man came out carrying a wooden crate.

"Ah, yes," said Tía Chela, standing up. "Please put that over on the table by the desk."

When the man had gone, the children gathered around the crate. It looked like one of the crates that Dr. Iris kept her dinosaur bones in at her paleontology camp.

"You've come at the right time," said Tía Chela. "I think you are going to find this very interesting. Jessie, there is a small toolbox behind the desk. Can you bring it to me?"

Jessie brought her the toolbox. "On second thought, I think I'll have one of you do this," the professor said. "It's a little difficult to use tools while balancing with a cane." She took out a hammer and handed it to Henry.

20

"What's in there?" Benny asked.

"Something very unique," said Tía Chela. "But I must warn you, it may seem a bit strange."

Henry pried the lid off and set it on the desk. Tía Chela pulled out the packing material to reveal another box.

Violet was excited to see what was inside and also a little nervous.

"When you see it, I'd like you to tell me what you think it looks like," Tía Chela said. She set down the box very carefully and opened the lid. Inside lay a small object set in foam.

Violet gasped as she leaned over to look.

"It looks like an animal skeleton," Jessie said. "But there aren't any leg bones. There is only something that looks like a tail."

"It looks like the skeleton of a mermaid," Henry said.

"It can't be a mermaid. It's too little," Violet said. "And it's creepy!"

"It's very old," Tía Chela said. "More than three

hundred years old. And you are right, Henry. This is meant to be a mermaid skeleton."

"Meant to be?" asked Violet. "What does that mean?"

"Let's take the box to one of the library tables, and I'll explain," Tía Chela said. "Henry, can you go to the main desk and get the book I left there? It's titled *A Field Guide to Ocean Skates and Rays*."

When Henry brought the book over, Benny pointed at the strange, dark-gray creature on the cover. It looked like a fish in the shape of a kite. "What is that?" he asked.

"It's a stingray," the professor said. "Rays and skates are kinds of fish that have very flat bodies. Henry, can you look in the index for *guitarfish*?"

Henry found the right page. It showed a creature like the one of the front cover. Next to it was a picture of the creature's skeleton.

"Is the little thing in the box a guitarfish skeleton?" Jessie asked. "It doesn't match the picture exactly."

"It is," Tía Chela nodded. "But it has been altered.

Rays and skates have skeletons that aren't made of bone. They are made of cartilage. Do you know what that is?"

Benny and Violet shook their heads. Jessie reached over and touched Benny's nose. "You have cartilage in you. That's the softer part of the end of your nose. It's why you can move it back and forth."

"Exactly right," said Dr. Iris. "Humans have both cartilage and bone, but these sea creatures only have cartilage."

"Hundreds of years ago, some sailors began carving the cartilage of these creatures to look like strange creatures of the sea," Tía Chela explained. "They would sell them to people as curiosities. But many people thought they were real and started to collect them."

Violet shivered. "That's not a collection I would want."

"These even have a name," Tía Chela explained. "They are called Jenny Hanivers, though no one is quite sure where the name comes from. This is the second one we've been able to purchase this year. We've been very lucky. They are very rare."

"I'm glad the skeleton is fake," Violet said. "If there really are mermaids, I'm sure they'd be pretty, even their skeletons."

"What are you going to do with it?" Henry asked.

"I'm going to donate it to a museum," said Tía Chela. "But I wanted to show it to you. There are lots of rumors going around about mermaids on the island. I wanted you to know that not all of them are true."

Tía Chela looked up at a clock on the wall. "Oh my, I didn't know it was getting so late. I'll go check to see how dinner is coming along and buzz down once it's ready. You can look around a bit more if you'd like."

The children roamed through the library, looking for everything they could find about mermaids. Jessie found an old, dusty book with a mermaid on the cover. She read about a circus in Fiji that claimed to have a mermaid on display.

Henry found a story from China of a strange creature washing up on shore after a tsunami; people thought it was a mermaid. Violet even found a story about mermaids on an island off the coast of Ireland.

"There are stories from all over," said Benny.

"That is an interesting point for our program," Dr. Iris said. "Do you have a guess about why that might be?"

"Maybe there really are mermaids all over!" said Benny. "Ice mermaids and warm-water mermaids and red mermaids and purple mermaids."

Dr. Iris smiled. "Perhaps. Any other ideas?"

Henry thought back to the stories they had heard when they were investigating Bigfoot. Those stories had been from around the world too. "Maybe people told stories about faraway places because people didn't know what kinds of creatures lived there," he said. "So people were more likely to believe them."

"I didn't know there were fish shaped like kites until I got here," said Benny. "Are those real?"

Dr. Iris nodded. "Yes, those are real."

Jessie set down the book she was reading. "That explains some of the old stories about mermaids," she said. "But Tía Chela said there are new stories about mermaids on the island. How do we find out if those are true?"

Dr. Iris smiled. "To answer that question," she said, "we need to find where the stories are coming from. Then we need to investigate a little deeper."

As the children were putting their books back on the shelves, a young woman hurried down the stairs next to the elevator. She had short spiky hair and was wearing a white sundress and flipflops. There was a big box in her hand.

"Gina?" Dr. Iris said.

The woman was so startled to see Dr. Iris standing there that she jumped back and fell down. The box she was holding hit the floor.

Henry moved to pick it up, but the woman got to her feet and grabbed it. "Sorry, I forgot you were coming today. Can't chat now. I have to get this to the post office. Please tell the professor I'll be back soon!"

Before anyone could say a word, the woman darted down the steps leading to the parking area.

"That was Gina, my aunt's assistant," Dr. Iris said after the woman was gone. "She's not usually so... flustered."

"She must really want to get to the post office," Jessie said. "It's getting dark, so it must be closing soon."

"Still, I've never seen her in such a rush," said Dr. Iris.

The buzzer sounded once again, and Tía Chela's voice came over the intercom. "Dinner is ready!" she announced.

Dr. Iris turned to the Aldens. "I have a surprise for you later this evening, but maybe it's best to wait until after dinner. It seems as though all we've had is surprises since we've arrived. Are you children ready to eat?"

Benny rubbed his belly. "Now there's a question I can answer!"

CHAPTER 3

SHIMMERING SHAPES

When the table was set and everyone was seated, there was still one open chair. "Have you seen Gina?" asked Tía Chela. "I thought she was going to eat with us."

Dr. Iris told her about Gina going to the post office.

Tía Chela shook her head. "She didn't mention it to me earlier. She's been very distracted worrying about Antonio."

"Does she know him well?" asked Henry. "He

sounds like someone who keeps to himself."

"He isn't that way with everyone," said Tía Chela. "Gina loves creatures of the sea almost as much as he does. I know she has been hoping to get a chance to work with him on the island. I do hope Antonio is all right!"

"I'm sure he is," said Dr. Iris. "We'll be very interested to hear his stories."

"Oh, that reminds me! I must show you an old map we found of his island," said Tía Chela. "The handwriting on it is very old, but I am sure part of the island is labeled 'Mermaid Cove.' I've never heard Antonio mention such a place."

As they ate, Violet couldn't stop thinking about the skeleton they had seen. "Why would people believe mermaids were so tiny?" she asked.

"That is a good question," said Tía Chela. "When Jenny Hanivers were created, no one really knew what a mermaid looked like, so it was easier to believe that perhaps they were very small. What do you think of when you think of mermaids?" she asked Violet.

Violet told her about a story she had read where six princess mermaids lived in an underwater palace made of coral. One of the mermaids rescued a human boy from a ship that sank. "It's fun to think there might be underwater mermaid palaces," Violet said.

"I read a story about how mermaids were good singers," said Jessie.

"Oh, yes, there are many stories about mermaids sitting by the shore and singing," Tía Chela said. "Our stories today mostly show mermaids as nice creatures, but it wasn't always that way. Some older stories tell of mermaids who can raise storms with their singing. Other stories say that mermaids sing to lead sailors into dangerous waters, where the ships would be wrecked."

"I can't imagine mean mermaids," Violet said.

"Mermaids were thought of as dangerous creatures in many different places," Tía Chela said. "We have one old account here in the library from a traveler to Thailand. He was told by local sailors that mermaids bite."

"Biting mermaids!" Benny said. "That's awful!"

"That doesn't seem right," said Violet.

"I thought it was a rare story, but my cook just told me she's been hearing about it too, just this past week! Right here on the island. You might want to investigate that, Iris."

"It sounds like we came at just the right time," said Dr. Iris. "But first I plan on learning about a different mermaid legend on the island. One that is more like the kind Violet has just described. To do that, we're going on a tour after dinner."

"Tonight?" Benny said excitedly. He liked staying up late, especially for surprises.

"But how will we see them in the dark?" asked Violet.

Dr. Iris smiled. "Where we're going, the water provides the light. It's a lagoon not far from here called Mermaid City."

The children were excited to start exploring. Once everyone was finished eating and the dishes were done, they hurried to get ready. Then they piled into the car, and Dr. Iris started driving. The narrow road brought them past brightly colored buildings built onto the hillside.

As they got closer to the water's edge, Henry called out, "I think we just passed Gina!"

The others turned to look out the window. It was growing dark, but they could make out a girl in a white dress talking to someone in front of a fish market.

"She was still holding her box," said Jessie. "I guess she didn't make it to the post office after all."

"I knew she was leaving too late to make it in time," Dr. Iris said. "I wonder what she is doing down here by the docks."

They came to a sign with a picture of a mermaid, like the one they saw at the airport. Across the top were the words *Mermaid City*. Dr. Iris pulled into a parking lot.

After they were checked in, everyone got a life jacket and headed to a dock lined with kayaks. Each one had lights on the front and the back. "When it gets darker, these will make it easier to stay together," she explained. "Ready to see something amazing?"

"Ready!" Benny yelled.

"Benny, you'll ride with me. Violet and Jessie can go together, and since Henry is the oldest, he can go by himself."

Once everyone was ready, they paddled down a shallow river. Small trees grew right in the water, their roots twisting upward.

Violet wrinkled her nose. "What's that smell?"

"The smell is coming from the water around the mangrove trees," Dr. Iris explained. "Mangroves grow in swampy areas. When they lose their leaves, the leaves drop into the water around their roots and decay. That's what causes the stink. It smells like rotten eggs, doesn't it?"

"I've never smelled rotten eggs," Violet said. "But if that's how they smell, I never want to!"

"You wouldn't, but many other creatures and plants don't mind it," Dr. Iris said. "The root systems are the perfect homes for fish, crabs, and shrimp. They also are nurseries for fish."

"Nurseries? Like for babies?" Benny asked.

"Yes, for baby fish," she said. "Many ocean fish that live around coral reefs begin their lives here. They stay here until they are old enough to move to the reef. Manatees also like mangroves."

Violet remembered her friend Katharine's purple stuffed manatee. "I hope we see a real one!" she said.

As it grew darker, the Aldens could just make out a line of kayaks in front of them from a tour group. Insects among the mangroves were buzzing, but there were no other noises except the soft sound of the paddles dipping into the water.

"I see lights up ahead," Jessie said. "But they aren't coming from the boats. It looks like they are coming from—"

"Underwater!" said Benny.

"Welcome to Mermaid City," Dr. Iris said as they paddled along. "Turn out the lights on your kayaks and look down as you paddle."

Jessie turned out the lights on their boat, and Violet let her paddle drift in the water for a moment.

All around it, blue light glowed and then dimmed. "It's so pretty!"

"Look!" a girl in a nearby kayak called. "I see something moving! Something big!"

The Aldens paddled toward the girl's kayak. Glowing shapes darted by the boat, leaving trails of light behind them.

"I think that was a school of fish," Henry said quietly.

"Do the fish light up too?" Benny asked.

"No, but they make the water move," said Dr. Iris. "And that's what makes the critters in the water light up."

It reminded Jessie of the lights that turn on outside their house when something moves past. "Why do they light up?" she asked. "Are they signaling to each other?"

"There are a number of theories about that," Dr. Iris said. "One is that they do it to find each other or to stay together. When the water moves, they could drift apart, so they light up to know which way to

move. These critters are very small, and the ocean is very big. Can you think of a creature that lives on land that can light up?"

"You mean like a type of squirrel or something?" Benny asked.

"Smaller than a squirrel," Dr. Iris said. "Think creature, not necessarily an animal."

"I know! Fireflies!" Violet said.

"Good, Violet!" Dr. Iris said. "Scientists think fireflies light up to find each other. Maybe these little creatures do too. And they aren't the only ocean critters like this. In very deep parts of the ocean, there is very little sunlight, so the things that live there make their own light!"

Another school of fish swam by, close to the Aldens' kayaks. As they passed, their scales shimmered in the blue light.

"I can almost imagine those fish were a mermaid, the way the water lit up as they moved their tails," Violet said.

"Imagine hundreds of years ago, before people

understood there were such things as microscopic creatures," Dr. Iris said. "The blue light must have looked like magic."

"Like an underwater city," said Jessie.

"Exactly!" said Dr. Iris.

They kayaked around the lagoon some more, admiring the lights in the water and the different kinds of fish they could see. As they went, Violet imagined actual mermaids swimming by, just out of sight. She liked the idea of an underwater city lit up by tiny creatures.

After they had circled the lagoon, Dr. Iris said, "Time to head back. We have a long day of investigating tomorrow."

Violet wished they could stay longer. But Dr. Iris's words made her remember the other things they had learned that night, about the missing professor and the not-so-nice mermaid stories. As they paddled out of the lagoon, Violet hoped that the rest of their investigation could be as peaceful as their trip to Mermaid City. But she had a feeling it might not be.

CHAPTER 4

A DIFFERENT KIND
OF STORY

At breakfast the next morning, Tía Chela didn't join them until they were almost finished. She looked worried.

"I'm sorry," she said. "Eric, the boat captain, can't leave as early as I had hoped. He took some tourists out for a sunrise cruise. I thought leaving early would be better so you'd have plenty of time, but we'll adjust. Gina is still planning to go with you to the island. She said she'd meet you at the harbor."

"Gina seems like she has a lot of errands to run," said Jessie. "We haven't gotten to talk to her at all."

"A little delay won't be a problem," Dr. Iris said. "We can do some more planning for our program. I wanted to show the children some of the old sea maps we have here."

"What a wonderful idea," said Tía Chela. "That reminds me, I need to show you that map of Antonio's island."

When they were finished with breakfast, the children followed Dr. Iris to a room next to the library. The room was filled with maps. Some looked very old and were drawn by hand.

"There's a strange-looking creature on this one," Jessie said. "Did the mapmakers draw in creatures they'd never seen?"

"That doesn't seem right," Henry said. "I thought maps were supposed to help people."

"When these maps were drawn, no one could explore what was beneath the surface of the ocean," Dr. Iris said. "So they imagined all sorts of things. For a long time, people believed that every land animal had an animal like it that lived in the ocean. They thought there were sea dogs, sea pigs, sea wolves. Some of these are now the names of real animals, like sea lions."

"Sea wolves sound scary," said Benny. "I'd rather see a sea giraffe. Or a sea camel."

Violet looked closely at her map. "There's a mermaid on this one! And some scary sea monsters too." She pointed. "That one looks like the creature Katharine drew, except it's even more scary! It's got three heads!"

"Yes, the lusca is a very old creature of legend," Dr. Iris said. "It's on my list of creatures to include in our program."

"Why did people make up stories of sea monsters?" Violet asked. "Not everyone likes scary stories."

"And why would they say they saw something when they didn't?" said Benny. "That's a lie."

"I have an idea about that," said Dr. Iris. "Many sailors could have imagined they saw something, especially if they were tired or in the middle of a storm, or, even worse, a hurricane. Sailing the ocean was very dangerous long ago. If a boat got lost or damaged, the sailors might be on the water far longer than they planned. They could even run out of food or fresh water. If a person doesn't have food or water for a long time, they can start to hallucinate. Do you know what that means?"

Benny shook his head.

"It means they start to imagine things that aren't there," Henry explained. "Do you think they could have imagined these sea monsters?"

"Possibly," Dr. Iris replied. "Think about if you were very sick and didn't know when you would get back to land. You'd be scared, so you might imagine all sorts of terrible creatures out to get you. There may be other reasons though."

Jessie thought for a moment. "I have an idea. A long time ago, a lot of people couldn't read or write, so if someone liked to make up stories, they'd have to tell them to people. Maybe it was exciting for the storyteller to see if they could get people to believe them."

"That's a good theory," Dr. Iris said. "I've never thought of that one before."

"They could have told stories for other reasons too," said Henry. "If they wanted people to visit someplace, they might tell stories about how great it was there."

Violet remembered the boat tour the night before. "Kind of like Mermaid City," she said. "We didn't see any mermaids, but the pictures on the signs make a lot of people want to go there."

"Good point," said Henry. "I guess if you wanted people to stay away, you could put scary looking monsters on the map too."

"Some of these drawings sure would keep me away," said Violet.

Tía Chela came into the map room holding a folder. She opened it on the table to reveal an old, yellow-looking map. "This is the map of Antonio's island I was telling you about."

"It looks like a peanut!" Benny said.

Tía Chela smiled. "You're right. The island is in the shape of a peanut. The part that dips in is the bay where Antonio keeps his boat. It's got a beautiful beach. This is the part that surprised me." Tía Chela pointed to one end of the island. "I didn't know there was a beach here, and it even looks like there is a cave in the rocks next to the beach. I think it's labeled 'Mermaid Cove,' but Gina says she doesn't think that's it. She says she can't make it out. I don't know. My eyesight isn't as good as it once was."

Jessie leaned in to try to make out the words next to the hidden beach. "It's very hard to read," she said.

"There's a magnifying glass in the desk drawer. You can see the lettering much better with it."

Henry got the magnifying glass. "Yes, the lettering is old and faded, but I think it does say Mermaid Cove," he said.

"I thought so!" Tía Chela said. "I think I should tell Gina she needs to get her eyes checked. She seemed so sure that it said something else."

"Do you think someone named it that because they saw mermaids there?" Benny asked.

"You will have to ask Antonio about that," Tía Chela said. "I'd send the map with you, but I'm afraid it's too fragile. I am hoping he will come here to look at it. Then we can decide what to do with it."

"I'll tell him about it when we find him," Dr. Iris said. "Speaking of which, we'd better get going."

"I do hope he is all right," Tía Chela said. "Let me know as soon as you can. And remember, he seems gruff when you first meet him, but he really doesn't mean it. He's a very nice person."

When the Aldens and Dr. Iris reached the harbor, they saw a boy standing at the entrance to the boat ramps. He waved a brochure and called, "Sign up for the Lusca Cruise tomorrow night. We're going on a sea monster hunt! Are you brave enough?"

The Aldens walked over to him, and he pointed to the brochure. The image looked very much like the creature Katharine had drawn—a shark's head on a body like an octopus.

"One has been sighted very near here." The boy motioned excitedly. "It came up out of the deep and attacked a fishing boat. The boat was nearly dragged underwater! Sign up and come look for it with us! It could be the most exciting trip you've ever taken!"

Dr. Iris smiled and took a brochure. "Who saw this creature?

"A friend of my father's cousin," the boy said. "He swears he saw it."

"He did? That's very interesting," she said. "Do you know the man's name? We'd like to talk to him."

"No," the boy said. Just then another group got out of a car, and the boy ran over to them, telling them about the boat tour.

"It seems like this lusca tour is pretty popular," Henry said, looking at the crowd around a big black boat. "And Katharine's grandfather was visiting for the same reason. I thought stories of scary monsters were supposed to keep people away. This one seems to be bringing more people in."

"Not me." Violet shivered thinking about the picture on the brochure.

"I want to check in with the harbormaster before we depart," said Dr. Iris. "Tía Chela told me he is friends with Doc Pez. Maybe he's heard something."

The harbormaster was on the phone when they went into his office. He waved at them and then pointed to some chairs by the wall while they waited. Dr. Iris sat down, but Violet looked at a large map on the wall. "This doesn't look like a regular map," she said. "Why are all the mountains colored blue?"

Henry walked over to look at it too. "Because those mountains are underwater. It's a map of the ocean floor," he said.

"I didn't know there were mountains underwater," Benny said. "Is that where sea mountain goats live?"

Dr. Iris laughed. "I haven't heard of those, Benny. But there are definitely mountains underwater. It's hard to believe, but Puerto Rico is actually the top of a mountain."

Benny looked down at his feet. "We're on top of a mountain right now?"

"That's strange to think about," said Violet. "Why is this part of the map such a dark blue? And this little part purple?"

"That dark blue and purple show where it is very deep," Dr. Iris said. "Not many people know this, but we're not far from the deepest point in the Atlantic Ocean. It's called the Puerto Rico Trench. It's so deep that if you could move Mount Everest and set it on the ocean floor, the part that was left sticking out of the water would be just a hill."

"Wow," Henry said. "It's hard to imagine how deep that is."

The harbormaster hung up the phone. "What can I do for you folks?" he said.

Dr. Iris introduced herself. "Have you heard from Antonio Amador lately?" she asked. "My aunt, Marcela Reyes, told me you are a friend of his. She's worried about him out there all alone."

The man gave a little laugh. "I wouldn't call him a

friend, exactly. But he puts up with me more than he does most people. I haven't heard from him, but I'm sure he's fine. Probably just in a grouchy mood and doesn't want to see anyone."

"We're going out to his island to look for him," Dr. Iris said. "I'll let you know when I get back why he hasn't been in."

The harbormaster went back to his desk. "Come to think of it, he hasn't picked up his mail in quite a while. I keep it here for him." The harbormaster paused. "You know, that *is* odd. I wonder what's happened to him?"

CHAPTER 5

OUT AT SEA

I'm glad you are going out to check on Antonio," the harbormaster said. "He's got quite a stack of mail here." He pulled out a big stack of letters with a rubber band around them. "Will you take these out to him?"

"Yes, we'll bring them," Dr. Iris said. "Can you tell us where the *Sea Dog* is berthed? That's the boat we are going out on."

The harbormaster gave them directions. Just as he

finished, the phone rang again, and he waved good-bye as he went to answer it.

Outside the office, the Aldens ran into Gina, who was hurrying down the boardwalk. She frowned when she saw them. "You really don't have to go," she said. "I told Professor Reyes I could go on my own. Doc Pez is not going to like extra people on the island."

"We want to go," Dr. Iris said. "And I'm sure he won't mind us for a few hours. Besides, we want to talk to him about his stories."

"All right, but I'm coming with," said Gina. Together, they walked along the line of boats. Henry spotted the *Sea Dog* first. It was a white boat with a large, old-fashioned steering wheel and a not-so-old-fashioned motor on the back.

A man wearing a billowy white shirt and a bandanna around his head waved at the group as they walked down the dock. He was very tan with long blond hair and a beard that was almost white, which was twisted into little braids.

"He looks like a pirate!" Benny said.

"He dresses that way for fun," Dr. Iris said. "Tourists like it."

"Hello, Iris," the captain said when they reached the boat. "It's been a long time. I've heard about your television show. It sounds very exciting."

"We think it will be. Eric, these are my helpers." Dr. Iris introduced the children and Gina.

"Welcome to the *Sea Dog*. I hope your aunt told you we've been having a little trouble with the boat," Eric said to Dr. Iris.

"No, she didn't say anything."

"Some engine trouble, on and off," Eric said. "I haven't figured out the problem yet. I told Professor Reyes I would find her someone else to go check on Antonio, but she insisted I go. She said the others don't like him well enough to bother. Not that I like him that much myself."

"Why not?" Gina asked. She sounded upset. "He's a very smart man."

"He may be smart, but he is such a cranky fellow.

And he really doesn't like us tourist boat operators. He ran me off the bay in front of his beach last year. We didn't even touch foot on shore!"

"He hates having tourists on the island," Gina said. "They throw their trash everywhere and act like they own the place."

"Not the people on my tours," Eric said. "Anchoring in the bay isn't going to do any damage to the island. I make sure we take all our trash with us."

"Being in the bay can cause more damage than you know," Gina said. She huffed and disappeared onto the boat.

"Don't mind her," Dr. Iris told Eric. "She's just worried about her friend. Now, I need to make some phone calls about our television program. I'm afraid once we're out on the water, I won't get a good signal. I'll be right back."

While the children waited on the dock, a large yacht pulled up. A girl in a purple swimsuit stood on the deck.

"It's Katharine!" Violet said. She waved and

yelled, "Katharine!"

Katharine smiled and waved back. "Hi, Aldens! I can't believe you're here!"

As soon as the boat docked, she jumped off and ran over to them. "Are you having fun? We are! I love sleeping on a boat. What are you doing here?"

"We're going out to an island to check on someone," Jessie said. "He hasn't been in touch for a while. His friends are worried."

"Oh, I hope he's okay," said Katharine. "We're just here for a little while. My grandfather has to meet someone. He says he's buying something really amazing, but he won't tell me what it is. He says I'll have to see it to believe it."

A man came down the dock carrying a small wooden box. Katharine's grandfather got off the boat to meet him.

"That must be him!" Katharine said. She ran over to her grandfather.

The man spoke to Katharine's grandfather for a few moments and then opened the box. Katharine peered inside then took a step back.

"Come look!" Katharine called to them. "You won't believe it."

The Aldens walked over. The man with the box frowned at them and held the box close. It seemed like he didn't want them to see inside.

"It's a little mermaid skeleton!" Katharine cried.

Inside the box, the Aldens saw some straw and a piece of burlap. On top of the burlap lay a little skeleton like the one they'd seen at Tía Chela's house.

Violet looked at it carefully. There was something different about it than the one they'd seen at Tía Chela's, but she couldn't figure out exactly what.

"I'm sorry, Katharine, but that's not real," Henry said. He explained what they'd learned from Tía Chela about Jenny Hanivers.

"Of course it's real," the man holding the box said. "It came from an island called Isla de la Lusca, not far from the Puerto Rico Trench."

"The island we are going to is by the Puerto Rico Trench," said Jessie, thinking back to the map in the harbormaster's office. "It's called Isla de la Reina."

The man's face grew serious. "The islands by the trench can be very dangerous. The woman I bought this from told me there have been reports of something dangerous in the water—mermaids."

"We went on a tour of the lagoon last night," said Violet, "and the lagoon mermaids were supposed to be nice."

"Not these ones. The mermaids of the deep are said to get angry when people come too close. They can even bite!"

Jessie looked over at the *Sea Dog*. She wanted to call Gina over to take a look, but Gina wasn't anywhere in sight. "Well, I don't know about the stories," Jessie said. "But I know someone who can tell you about the skeleton. Let me go find her."

"I have to be going," the man said. "Do you want it or not?" he asked Katharine's grandfather.

"Very interesting," said Katharine's grandfather. "How much?"

"Five hundred dollars," the man said.

"Two hundred."

"This is very rare," the man said. "I could easily sell it to someone else. But because I need some cash today, I'll sell it to you for three hundred."

"Two hundred fifty. That's my final offer."

The man sighed. "All right, but you are getting a deal." He handed over the box. Katharine's grandfather took out his wallet and gave the man some money, and the man hurried off down the boardwalk.

"Do you really believe it's a mermaid skeleton?" Henry asked.

Katharine's grandfather laughed. "It doesn't matter what I believe," he said. "It makes a good story. I'll take it around with me on book signings. People will be thrilled to see something like this."

"I believe it!" Katharine said. "Can we go look for the place where it came from? What was it called?"

"Lusca," Jessie said. "Isla de la Lusca."

"Yes, that means island of the lusca," Katharine's grandfather said. "I'll have to get on the radio and see if someone can give me coordinates to find it.

Sounds like a good day for an expedition. Katharine, let's go get you some more sunscreen so we can take off again."

Katharine waved at the Aldens as she and her grandfather walked away. "Maybe we'll see you again!" she called.

The Aldens went back to the boat. Gina was sitting on one of the chairs near the back.

"There you are," said Jessie. "Did you hear? That man just sold a Jenny Haniver. I was hoping you could explain it wasn't real. They didn't believe us when we tried to tell them."

Gina shook her head. "I didn't hear. Sorry, I went below deck to look around."

"It's strange," Henry said. "Dr. Iris told us they are very rare. But now we've heard about them two days in a row."

"Maybe there are more of them than Dr. Iris thinks," Gina said.

"Or maybe they really are skeletons!" said Benny. "What if the story that man told was true?"

"Gina, do you think there could be something hiding in the waters by the trench?" asked Violet.

Gina looked uncomfortable. It was clear she did not want to answer Violet's question. "We have more important things to worry about," she said. "Like finding Doc Pez."

Just then, Eric came back onto the deck with an armful of life jackets, followed by Dr. Iris. Eric went over some safety instructions. Then he went to turn on the engine. The motor sputtered a few times, but then it cranked on.

Soon they were out on the open ocean. The boat picked up speed, and before long, it was cutting through the water, going very fast.

Violet and Benny crouched at the boat's railing and watched the sparkling blue water go by. It was beautiful. But as Violet looked into the water, she also thought about just how far down it went. Gina had not answered her question about whether there could be something hiding in the deep waters of the trench. Did she know something that she wasn't telling them?

The boat came across some waves and began to bounce up and down. Eric slowed the engine. But as the boat bobbed, a mooring rope came undone and began to unspool into the water.

"Grab onto the rope," Eric called. "We don't want it to get caught in the engine."

Jessie picked up the rope from the deck and began to pull it back in. In the meantime, Eric quickly throttled down the engine and turned it off. Soon the boat was at a complete stop.

Once Jessie had pulled in the rope, Eric apologized. "I should have secured that better before we went out. Oh well. No need to worry."

But when Eric tried to start the engine back up, it just sputtered. He tried two more times. Nothing happened. He gave a big sigh and lifted the hatch of the engine compartment.

Violet looked at the smoke that came out of the engine compartment. Then she looked out over the open water. There was no sight of land anywhere. "Should we be worried now?" she asked.

CHAPTER 6

SOMETHING IN THE WATER

I can fix it," Eric said. "And if for some reason I can't, we have a radio and can call for help. It's not like the old days when we'd have to wait for someone to come along. Jessie, since you are closest to the cabin, will you go get my toolbox?"

Henry gave a whistle at the sight of the all the parts inside the engine compartment. "That looks complicated," he said.

"It's not so bad once you get used to it," Eric said.

"But I just can't figure out what's wrong."

The captain worked on the engine for what seemed like a long time.

Dr. Iris could tell Violet and Benny were getting worried. "Why don't we have lunch while we're waiting?" she suggested.

At the mention of food, Benny brightened up, and Violet nodded. She was happy to have something to do.

Dr. Iris got out the cooler, and everyone took sandwiches and drinks. "These sandwiches are my favorite. They are called *tripletas* because they have three meats. They are a popular Puerto Rican sandwich. And for dessert, we have cookies."

Benny was excited to try something new, but when he took a bite, he covered his mouth. His eyes got big. "This is spicy!" he said. He took out the piece of sausage and tossed it over the edge.

"Sorry, I should have warned you about that," Dr. Iris said. "I guess I've eaten too many of these. I'm used to the spice."

"That's okay," said Benny. "Now it's a *doubleta*—two meats!"

As the children ate their lunch, Dr. Iris glanced at her watch. "What is it?" said Henry.

"Oh, nothing," she said. "I just hope we find Antonio right away. I'm afraid we may not be able to get back today if we don't get on our way soon."

"We wouldn't have to stay on the boat, would we?" asked Violet. She didn't like the idea of spending the night far out at sea.

Before Dr. Iris could answer, a splash came from beside the boat. The children hurried to the edge.

"I don't see anything," said Henry. "It might have just been a wave."

"That's no wave," said Benny. "Look! It's a fin!"

Sure enough, a large gray fin stuck out of the water next to the boat. It was coming right toward them.

"What is it?" asked Violet. "It's going to attack our boat!"

"I don't think that is what it's after," said Dr. Iris.

She did not sound worried, which made Violet feel a little bit better.

Suddenly a dolphin's head rose up out of the water with its mouth open. It was not taking a bite of the boat. Instead, it swallowed up the sandwich meat that Benny had thrown overboard. Then it made a happy squeaking noise and swam away.

Henry mussed Benny's hair. "I don't think the dolphin thought the sandwich meat was too spicy. He seemed to like it."

Violet laughed. She was glad it had just been an animal looking for food. Still, she jumped when the sound of the engine roared to life.

"We're back in business!" Eric called.

Once the boat was moving again, it didn't take long before Henry spotted a small island in the distance. "Is that our destination?" he asked.

"We're going to pass a few more before we get to Doc Pez's island," the captain said. "There are about a hundred small islands around Puerto Rico."

"I didn't know that," said Jessie. "Are we close to

the Puerto Rico Trench?"

"We're headed that way," Eric said. "Just past Doc Pez's island, the depth really starts to drop off."

"It's scary to think of really deep water," Violet said. "A boy on the dock was talking about luscas. He said there was a place called Isla de la Lusca where one attacked a man's boat. They're taking tourists out there to look for it."

Eric let out a whoop of laughter. "That story! Serves old Doc Pez right."

"What do you mean?" Jessie asked. "What does Doc Pez have to do with the story?"

"He's the one who told it!" Eric said.

"Really?" said Benny. "Did he see it happen?"

Eric shook his head. "I heard from the harbormaster that Doc Pez came up with an idea a couple years ago to keep tourists away from his island. He thought if he spread a story that there was a sea monster there, people would stay away. Sounds like it's going to do just the opposite."

"But the boy said the island was called Isla de

la Lusca. That's not the name of the island where Antonio lives," Dr. Iris said.

"He made up the name too!" Eric chuckled. "He thought it sounded more frightening than Isla de la Reina, which means 'Island of the Queen.' I heard he even tried to get the name changed."

"That's where Katharine and her grandfather are going—Isla de la Lusca," Violet said. She explained how they knew Katharine and about seeing her at the dock. "Maybe we'll see them there."

"The man who sold them the Jenny Haniver artifact told them it came from Isla de la Lusca too," Henry added.

"What? What's this about a Jenny Haniver?" Dr. Iris looked surprised.

Henry told her about the man on the docks who sold the artifact.

"I can't believe it," Dr. Iris said. "Where would someone get something like that? Gina, did you see it? Gina?"

Gina had been sitting at the front of the boat

looking off into the distance. When she heard Dr. Iris, she just shook her head.

"Well, I hope it's not stolen from somewhere," Dr. Iris said. "I'll check on that when we get back. If it was taken from a museum, it will be in the news."

"The man with the Jenny Haniver said there were biting mermaids around the island," Violet said to Dr. Iris, "just like Tía Chela was talking about."

Eric gave another whoop of laughter. "Biting mermaids? Now that's a new one for me. Though it does make a good story."

Violet looked over the edge. The water was much darker than it had been close to the shore. She wasn't sure what to believe about the legendary creatures of the deep. "Do you think the stories could be true?" she asked Eric.

"I don't think there are giant sea creatures that attack boats," he said. "I do believe there are sea creatures that haven't been discovered yet, especially in the deepest parts of the ocean. Almost every year scientists find new things. I remember reading about a sea creature everyone thought had been extinct for millions of years—something called a coelacanth. These people diving along a coral reef just saw one swim by one day. Can you imagine?"

Violet looked back at the dark water. "I wonder what else might be down there that we don't know about," she said.

"The island is up ahead," said Eric, pointing out over the water. "It looks like there's another boat already in the bay."

"Is it Doc Pez's boat?" asked Henry.

Eric shook his head. "It looks like a yacht."

"That's Katharine's grandfather's boat," Jessie said. She saw something splashing in the water next to the boat. "I think someone is in the water!"

CHAPTER 7

MISSING

As they got closer, the children could hear Katharine calling out. "I think something bit me!" she said, flailing about in the water.

"Swim to the boat," her grandfather called back.

Katharine didn't seem to be listening, so her grandfather went to the edge of the boat and started to climb over.

"We can help her," Jessie called as their own boat approached. "Can we jump in?" she asked Eric.

He turned off the motor. "Yes, go ahead."

"Wait!" said Benny. "You don't know what could be out there!"

Jessie scanned the shallow water. "There's nothing here, Benny. Don't let those stories of sea monsters worry you. They are just stories. Everything will be okay."

Benny wasn't so sure. But before he could say another word, Jessie and Henry jumped into the water and started swimming toward their friend.

"My foot really hurts!" Katharine said when they reached her. "Do you see what bit me? I don't want it to bite you."

Henry and Jessie looked down into the water. "Whatever it was is gone now," Jessie said.

"You should get out of the water so we can see how bad it is," Henry said. "Come on, we'll swim with you."

The three made their way back to her grandfather's yacht. Jessie and Henry helped Katharine climb up the swim ladder.

Benny and Violet watched from the *Sea Dog*. "I don't see any fish," Benny said. "Do you think it was a mermaid?"

"We'd be able to see a mermaid too," said Violet, though she was unsure what to make of the situation herself. "And Katharine wasn't doing anything but swimming. Why would that make a mermaid angry?"

Eric called out to Katharine's grandfather, who was examining the girl's foot. "It's probably a jellyfish sting," he said. "It's not uncommon, but at least it won't hurt for long. I always carry vinegar to put on jellyfish stings. I'll get it."

Henry got back in the water and swam over to get the vinegar. Then he brought it back to the yacht.

"It feels better," Katharine said as her grandfather dabbed the vinegar on a small red spot on her foot. "But it did really hurt at first."

"How did you end up in the water?" asked Violet. "Did you fall in?"

Katharine grabbed onto Winston, the stuffed animal she'd had on the plane. "I was sure I saw a manatee down there. I went to the edge to take a closer look. That's when something seemed to hit the boat, and I fell in."

"Something hit the boat?" asked Henry. "Are you sure?"

"I think I've been telling you too many stories, kiddo," said Katharine's grandfather. "I think we hit a big wave."

"I've read jellyfish stings are painful," Jessie said. "I can understand how you would think it was a bite."

"Well, that was enough excitement for a little while," Katharine's grandfather said. "Thank you for helping, Aldens. Katharine, how about we call it a day? It took longer than I thought to get here. I'd like to get back to the harbor before dark."

Henry and Jessie said good-bye to Katharine and swam to the *Sea Dog*. They climbed aboard, and everyone waved as the yacht headed out of the bay. Katharine had Winston in her hand. She raised the manatee and pretended it was waving at them too.

"I should have asked to see that Jenny Haniver,"

Dr. Iris said. "I wish they hadn't left right away."

"It wasn't a very good fake," Gina said. "It had what looked like feet instead of a tail."

Gina hadn't talked for most of the trip, so the children were surprised to hear her speak up. So surprised they did not think to ask how she knew about the Jenny Haniver. After all, she'd been on the boat when the man had shown it to Katharine's grandfather at the docks.

After a little while, Jessie spoke up again. "Katharine said she was looking for manatees, but when she fell in, she must have been thinking about those terrible stories. That's why she thought she got bitten."

Dr. Iris nodded. "Once an idea gets in someone's head, it can make that person imagine all sorts of things."

"Can we pull into the dock?" Gina said impatiently. She pointed at a rickety wooden pier sticking out from a sandy beach. "We need to check on Doc Pez. His boat isn't here."

Eric gave a snort. "That boat is so old I'm surprised it still floats."

The *Sea Dog* glided right up next to the pier. Eric shut off the engine and tossed a looped rope around one of the cleats.

"That building on top of the hill is falling down," Violet said. "Is that Doc Pez's house?"

"No, that's an old lighthouse," Gina said. "Doc Pez lives through there." She motioned toward one end of the beach. They could just make out a path leading into a dense forest.

"Let's leave our things on the boat until we know what's going on," Dr. Iris said.

On shore, the group followed an overgrown path through the trees and brush until they came to a clearing. At the back of the clearing sat a small wooden house with a large porch. Chickens were pecking in the dirt in front of the house. The birds ignored the group as they walked up to the house.

"Hello!" Dr. Iris called out, but no one answered.

As the group got closer, they noticed a chair on the porch. It had been tipped on its side.

"That's not a good sign," Henry said.

"Doc Pez, are you here?" Gina called.

No one answered. "The screen door isn't shut all the way," Jessie said when they climbed the steps up onto the porch.

Gina reached the door first, but when she touched the handle, she jerked her hand away and wiped it on her shorts. "Eww! It has something slimy on it."

"Slimy?" said Benny. "From what?"

Dr. Iris used one finger to take hold of the handle. She held it open so everyone else could go inside.

"Doc Pez?" Gina called again.

"What happened here?" Jessie asked. She pointed to a sofa. A pillow had been ripped, and the stuffing was scattered on the floor.

"I don't know," Dr. Iris said.

Benny reached down and picked up a picture frame. Gina took it from him. "That's me and some other students with Doc Pez." She pointed to a stocky man with white hair and a white beard. He was dressed in old khaki shorts and a faded shirt. "I wish I knew where he was," Gina said. She sounded like she was about to cry.

"We'll find him," said Henry.

Violet moved toward a door leading to another room. When she looked inside, she backed away, her mouth wide open.

"What is it?" Henry asked.

"There's…There's something in here!"

"Oh dear," Dr. Iris said.

Everyone crowded in the doorway. Inside, a brown and white animal was munching on something on the floor.

"A goat!" said Benny, a bit relieved.

"It looks like he's eating a mango," said Henry. Several bits of fruit lay on the table and floor, along with a wooden bowl.

"It doesn't seem scared of us," Jessie said.

"No, Doc Pez treats his goats like children," Gina said, wiping her hand on her shorts again. "I think the goop on the door handle was goat slobber. It must have used its mouth to pull the door open."

"Yuck!" Violet said.

A loud braying noise came from behind the house. Benny jumped. "What's that?"

"That's another goat," Gina said. "Doc Pez usually has four or five."

"Let's try to get this one out of here and back with its friends," said Henry. He picked up the piece of fruit from the floor. "I bet he'll want this last piece."

The goat turned and watched Henry.

"Come on. It's tasty." Henry held the mango close to the goat's nose, and the animal took a step forward.

Henry took a step back and then another as the goat followed him out of the kitchen, into the main room, and then out the door onto the porch. The others went after him, following him to the goat pens.

One pen stood empty, its gate open. Henry led the goat inside and then set down the mango. The goat started to munch, so Henry went out and closed the gate behind him.

"The water troughs are full," Jessie said, "and it looks like fresh water. That's a clue. Someone must have filled them recently. Unless it has rained a lot in the last few days."

"There really isn't anyone else on the island?" Violet asked.

"No, just Doc Pez," Gina said. "Sometimes students come out to stay and do research, but we'd see their gear if they were here. I'm going to go check on the lighthouse. Dr. Pez has this silly idea that he can fix it up all by himself. Everyone tells him he should get help, but he won't listen."

"We can go with you," Henry offered.

"No, I can go faster myself," Gina said. "If Doc Pez isn't there, I don't know where else he'd be. The rest of the island is just forest and rocks." She hurried back around to the front of the house.

After Gina had gone, Henry turned to his siblings. "Gina said the rest of the island is forest and rocks, but that isn't right. There is another beach, remember? We saw it on the old map at Tía Chela's house. It was labeled Mermaid Cove, and there was a cave there too. Why didn't Gina mention that?"

"Gina is acting strange," said Jessie. "It seems like she might know more about what's going on than she is letting on."

"Maybe she's upset," said Benny. "I would be upset if my friend was missing."

"That's a good point, Benny," said Henry. "But I think the beach is worth checking out. Doc Pez might have slipped on a rock and hurt himself."

Or worse, Violet thought to herself. What if something had attacked him?

"All right, you should go look," Dr. Iris said. "But be careful. I'll go down to the beach and tell Eric the situation. I need to talk to him about our plan to get back to the mainland."

The Aldens followed a path through the trees and down to a rocky area. They called for Doc Pez, but no one answered. The path seemed to end right at a wall of rocks. To the right was a big drop that went down to the ocean.

"There must have been a rockfall," Violet said. "Maybe we should go back."

"Wait, there's more to the path." Jessie pointed to a narrow gap between two large rocks. "I think we should keep going. If Doc Pez came down this path, he may need our help."

CHAPTER 8

MERMAID COVE

Henry led the way through the gap in the rocks and down the narrow path. "Be careful," he warned. "It's steep."

They picked their way down the cliff and ended up on a small beach. Rocky outcrops lined each end, hiding it from the rest of the island. The beach would have been beautiful, except it was covered with garbage: plastic bottles and bags, netting, and even some flip-flops.

"This is terrible," Jessie said. "I wish we could clean this up, but we don't have anywhere to put the garbage."

"Who put all this here?" Benny asked.

Henry surveyed the beach. "I don't think anyone did," he said.

"What do you mean?" asked Violet. "Where did it come from then?"

"I think it's washing in from the ocean," said Henry. "I don't see any sign of Doc Pez or his boat though."

Jessie tried to remember the map at Tía Chela's. "The cave would be on the other side of those rocks. There was this beach, then a big rock, and then the mouth of the cave was just on the other side."

Henry walked over to the rocks. "We'll have to wade into the water to get there. It looks shallow enough though. I can go first and make sure it doesn't get any deeper." He went around and called back over his shoulder. "It's fine! Not deep at all."

Jessie held Benny's hand, and they followed Violet through the water.

Once they reached the other side, they could see a long way down another narrow strip of beach.

"No Doc Pez, but more garbage," Violet said.

"There really is a cave here!" Jessie said. She pointed at an arched section in the rocky outcropping behind them.

Benny stopped suddenly. "Wait!" he said. "Did anybody hear that?"

"Hear what?" Henry asked.

"Listen. There's a noise coming from the cave."

Everyone was quiet for a moment. "I hear it too," Violet said.

"Doc Pez?" Jessie called. "Are you in there?"

There was no answer, but the hissing noise continued.

Violet twisted her hands together. "What do we do?"

"We need to go in and look," Henry said.

Benny shook his head. "I don't think I want to go in there. We don't know what's making that sound. It could be a sea monster or even a mean mermaid!"

"I don't think either one of those things is in there," Jessie said. "Remember what Dr. Iris said? Once an idea gets in someone's head, it can make that person imagine all sorts of things. We've been talking about sea monsters and mermaids, so the idea is in your head. I say we go in and look."

"Okay," Benny said. "But I'm not going first."

They made their way slowly into the cave. The light became dimmer as they went, and they had to watch their steps along the uneven rocks. In the back of the cave was a large pool of water with a huge gray boulder in the middle. It was covered with a fishing net.

Jessie took a few steps farther into the cave and then stopped. "That's not a boulder. It's moving!"

There was another hissing noise, and everyone scrambled back to the entrance of the cave. "What was that?" Benny asked. "Are you sure it was moving?"

"It was moving," Violet said. "I saw it too."

Henry went a little way back into the cave. "I wish I had a flashlight," he said. "I've read about sea creatures getting trapped on beaches. Maybe that's what happened here. It got trapped in the cave and the net is making it hard for it to get out."

"Let's go look again," Jessie said. "Where we were standing before was blocking the light. If we stay to one side, we can see better."

They moved back into the cave. "It is some sort of sea creature," Henry said. "See, there's its tail and its flippers." The creature made another hissing sound, but it was not as loud.

"It's so big!" Violet said. "Is it a walrus?"

"Look at its head," Jessie said. "I think it's a manatee. It's a big, gray version of Winston. Its head is the shape of an elephant without a trunk. Poor thing. It must be awful to be trapped like this."

"Should we try to get the net off it?" Benny asked.

"I don't think so," Henry said. "Dr. Iris said they are gentle, but we don't want to scare it. It might get even more tangled up."

"We're going to have to go get help," Jessie said.

They waded back around the rocks and picked

their way through the garbage to the path. Benny thought he heard another sound, this one coming from the ocean. He looked back out at the water. "There's a boat out there!"

A man in a small boat was waving and yelling at them. The boat bobbed up and down in the waves. With each wave, the boat got pushed closer to shore.

"I think that's Doc Pez," Violet said. "He has white hair and a white beard just like the man in the photograph!"

"His boat must not be working," Henry said.

As the boat came closer, they could see the professor had hurt his right arm. He held it at his side and used a paddle with his left.

"He can't really paddle a boat like that in the ocean, can he?" Violet asked.

"No," Henry said. "The boat is getting pushed toward the rocks. I think he's going to try to use the paddle to keep from hitting them."

"We can wade out and help him," Jessie said.

"Yes, Violet and Benny, you'd better stay on the

beach," Henry said. "We shouldn't go too deep without life jackets. We'll have to wait until the boat comes close enough to catch hold of it." They positioned themselves between the rocks and the boat.

"Grab the paddle when I get close enough," the man yelled. "I'll throw a rope to the other one of you."

Luckily, the boat was so small Jessie and Henry were able to keep it from hitting the rocks. The two pulled the boat toward the beach. Violet and Benny ran out to help.

"I need a hand getting out," the man said. Even with Henry and Jessie helping him, the man had trouble getting out of the boat. Once he was on the beach, he leaned against the boat and took a few deep breaths.

"Climb in and get some more ropes," he said to Henry. "We'll tie the boat on both sides to rocks so it can't drift one way or the other. Can you help me drag it partway up on the beach?"

Everyone helped, but they still struggled to get the boat far enough up on the beach so it wouldn't be pulled out again. When it was up far enough, the man raised his hand. "Okay, we can stop."

He leaned against the boat again to catch his breath. Violet noticed he was wearing a necklace made of pink beads knotted on a string. The beads were oval and shimmered a little when the sunlight hit them. The man saw her looking at them. He said, "Now who are you, and what are you doing on my island?" He sounded very gruff.

"We're here with Dr. Iris Perez," Jessie said. "You're Antonio, aren't you? She came to check on you because her aunt was worried about you. You have to help—"

"Worried about me?" the man said, interrupting Jessie. "What nonsense. Where is Iris?"

"She's back at your house," Henry said. "But please, we need to tell—"

He interrupted again. "Well, we'd better go tell her I'm fine, and then you can all leave."

"There's a manatee stuck in the cave!" Benny said very fast, before the man could speak again.

"What?" Doc Pez stared at Benny. Benny repeated himself.

"It's trapped in a fishing net," Violet said. "We don't know how to help it."

"So that's where Flor is!" the man exclaimed. "I've been looking for her for days!"

"Flor?" Henry asked. "The manatee has a name?"

"Yes, well, I named her that," said Doc Pez. "I don't know what her family calls her."

Henry and Jessie shared a confused look. Doc Pez continued, "It's easier to monitor them if I give them names." He headed toward the rocks where the cave was located. "I've been keeping track of them ever since they came back here. They were gone for years, but now they've returned to feed on the north side of the island. I saw Flor trapped in that net at the feeding ground. But she disappeared before I could get to her." He splashed out into the water and wobbled a little bit as if he was about to lose his balance.

Henry ran after him. "Do you want some help getting around the rocks?"

"No, no," Doc Pez said. "It's just this arm is making everything difficult. I might need some help with Flor." He stopped. "We're going to need a knife. You, what's your name?" he asked, pointing at Jessie. "Climb aboard the boat. There's a utility knife in the compartment on the passenger side. Go get that and bring it along."

Jessie ran and got the knife while Violet and Benny waited for her. Henry followed Doc Pez, staying close in case the man lost his balance.

"Violet, will you hold Benny's hand too?" Jessie said. "The water looks deeper now."

Benny took a few steps in and then stopped. "It is deeper," he said. "It's up to my knees."

"The tide is coming in," Doc Pez called back over his shoulder. "We need to hurry and get Flor untangled before it's all the way in. The water in the cave will be too deep for us then, but she'll be able to swim out."

They waded through the water until they reached the entrance to the cave. "I don't hear any hissing noises anymore," Henry said. "Is that the kind of noise manatees usually make?"

"Above water it is," Doc Pez said. "She's probably getting tired from struggling to get out."

The water in the cave had risen at least a foot, but the manatee was still in the same place as before. Doc Pez gave everyone directions on how they could help with the net. Then he began to cut away at the rope strands, talking to the manatee the whole time. He didn't sound gruff at all.

"She doesn't understand me, of course," he said. "But I've found it never hurts to talk to creatures."

As he worked, something in the back of the cave caught Violet's eye. It was shiny and pink. Violet thought it looked just like the beads on Doc Pez's necklace. But as she started to go toward it, Doc Pez finished cutting the rope from the manatee.

"We need to get out of here," said Henry. "The water is rising fast."

"I think I see something," said Violet. "I just need to get to the other side."

A wave came in and crashed against the back of the cave.

"There's no time!" Doc Pez said. "If we don't get out now, we'll be swimming!"

SWIMMING FREE

Benny nearly did have to swim, but Jessie and Henry kept hold of him as they went back to the beach.

Once they were there, Doc Pez stared at them, frowning. "This cave is a secret," he said. "Very few people know about it. If tourists found out about it, there would be crowds lining up to visit. Do you promise not to tell anyone?"

"We promise," Henry said. The others nodded.

Doc Pez glared at them again. "I just thought of something. How did you get on the island?" he asked. "Don't tell me Iris brought you out on a boat. I don't remember her being much of a water person. Who else is on my island?"

"Well, there is a woman named Gina," Jessie said. "She works for Dr. Iris's aunt, and she said she used to be one of your students."

"Oh, Gina, yes, of course. Excellent student. I don't mind her being here. Anybody else? I hope there isn't a whole horde of people roaming about the island that you haven't told me about."

"There is the boat captain, Eric, but he's down at his boat," Benny said.

The man rolled his eyes. "More people!"

"That's all though," Violet assured him.

"Hmm…I hope so. All right. Let's go see if you are telling the truth. I don't want to find anyone else lurking around."

Before the Aldens could make their way back up the cliff, a voice called out. "Henry! Jessie!" It was Dr. Iris.

"We're here!" Jessie called back. "And we found Doc Pez!"

Dr. Iris came down the path, followed by Gina and Eric. "Antonio, I'm so glad to see you," said Dr. Iris. "We were so worried about all of you. It's getting late."

The Aldens explained what had happened, though it took a while for them to get all the facts out.

"The manatee is still in there?" Dr. Iris said.

Doc Pez looked at his watch. "Yes, but the tide is almost all the way in. We should be seeing her swim out in a few minutes. If she doesn't come out, we'll have to think up a new plan."

"Where have you been?" Gina said to Doc Pez. "People are worried that they haven't seen you in so long."

"I hurt my arm, and I didn't want to make the trip until it was better." He explained about the boat too. "I don't know what's wrong with it," he said. "It worked fine for thirty years with only a few new parts here and there."

"I bet Eric could fix it," Benny said. "He fixed an engine on his boat, and that was really big. Your boat is little, so I bet the engine is little."

Doc Pez's eyes narrowed as he looked over at Eric. "I know you," he said, pointing his finger at the boat captain. "You're the one who keeps trying to bring tourists here to trash up the place. I'd recognize that pirate getup anywhere."

Eric stood up straight. "You should know that everywhere I take people, I make sure no trash is left behind," he said. "I did try to bring my tour here once, but you ran us off. Despite that, I would be happy to take a look at your boat."

"Why would you help me out?" Doc Pez asked suspiciously. "I'm still not going to let you bring tourists to the island."

Eric held up his hands. "I know you won't. I'm just trying to be friendly. I'd help out any boater with a problem."

Doc Pez didn't say anything for a few moments, but finally he waved in the direction of his boat. "All right. I'll let you take a look. Wait until we see if the manatee makes it out of the cave. I don't want her frightened by any engine noises."

"If Eric spends time on your boat, you're going to have to put us up for the night," Dr. Iris said. "Did anyone else notice it's getting dark?"

Doc Pez scowled. "I've never had children out on the island. They won't run around and yell all hours of the night, will they?"

"Have they been running around and yelling this afternoon?" Dr. Iris asked.

"No, I suppose not," Doc Pez said.

"Of course they haven't. Gina tells me you have some hammocks the graduate students use when they come out here. Do you think we could use them?"

"Yes. All right, you can stay. Just for one night though. Iris, you haven't told me why you are here in Puerto Rico. I thought you spent your time gadding about the world looking for dinosaurs."

"I told you—people were worried about you," said Dr. Iris.

"But why did you bring all these children out here?"

"We want to hear your mermaid story," Violet said.

Dr. Iris explained about the television program.

"Well, I suppose I could tell it to you if you are staying the night," Doc Pez said. He checked his watch. "But first we need to keep watch for Flor. It's almost high tide."

The group made their way back to the entrance of the cave. The water was coming much farther up on the beach than it had been before.

Benny was the first to spot something in the water. He grabbed hold of Doc Pez's sleeve. "There she is!" He pointed to what looked like a big gray rock in the shallow water.

"That's her all right," Doc Pez said.

"Why is she moving so slowly?" Violet asked. "Is she okay?"

"She is recovering. But manatees never move too quickly. That's why boats can be such a danger

to them. The creatures can't get out of the way fast enough." He looked over at his own boat. "It's getting too dark to take a look at the boat tonight," he said to Eric.

"I can look at it tomorrow morning," Eric said. "Let me just make sure it's secure for tonight."

While they waited, Violet looked around. "Why is there so much garbage here?" she asked. "It's too bad."

"This is the windward side of the island," Doc Pez said. "The strongest winds come from the east. They blow in garbage from all over the Atlantic. I come out here to collect it every week, but there is always more coming in."

"It's too much for one person," Gina said. "Some of the other students and I have been trying to raise money so you could have some help."

Doc Pez patted her on the arm. "I know. I've heard about that and I appreciate it, but you don't have to worry. I'll manage."

"All secure!" Eric called.

"Good," Doc Pez said. "I'd like to get back to my house and get something to eat. I've been out in that boat all day and I'm very hungry."

"I'm hungry too!" Benny said.

The group made its way up the path. Dr. Iris walked on the side of Doc Pez's good arm, in case he needed help.

"How did you hurt your arm, anyway?" she asked.

"It's the tourists' fault," Doc Pez grumbled. "Who else? One of the goats, Mofongo, got out, and some tourists spotted him. They were chasing after him trying to get a picture with him, of all things! What nonsense! Mofongo wasn't happy at all. While I was trying to catch up with them to tell them to leave him alone, I tripped. I can't stand tourists running all over the place like it's just here to be a background to their pictures."

"If Mofongo is the big goat, he got out again," Henry said.

"We found him in your kitchen," Violet added.

"And he chewed up a pillow," Dr. Iris said, "so if

you notice one missing, that's why."

Doc Pez sighed. "I suppose I can't blame him. I was gone a long time today. The goats are probably as hungry as Benny and me."

Once they were back at the house, Jessie helped Doc Pez make rice and beans. Eric went to get the cooler with the leftover food from lunch, and they settled down to eat.

"Can we hear the mermaid story now?" Violet asked when they were almost finished.

Doc Pez leaned back in his chair. "Yes, I am true to my word. But I would prefer if you kept this story out of your program."

CHAPTER 10

CASE CLOSED?

I n our family," Doc Pez began, "it is said that my great-great-grandmother was a mermaid who decided to become human."

Violet gasped.

"Really?" Benny asked.

"That's how the story goes," Doc Pez said. "My great-great-grandfather was a pirate, and after one journey, he brought home a beautiful woman with long hair as black as midnight. They married, but neither would ever say where they met or where she was from. She kept to herself and her family, and she was happy for the most part. Though, sometimes she would disappear for days at a time and come home dripping wet."

He reached his hand up to his necklace. "This belonged to her. We've always called these mermaid pearls because they're so rare only a mermaid could find them."

"I thought they were beads," Violet said.

"No, and though they aren't true pearls, they *are* formed inside a marine creature," Doc Pez said. "Do you know where pearls come from?"

"From oysters," Jessie said. "A grain of sand gets inside their shell. Since an oyster's body is very soft, the sand irritates it. Somehow, they can create a coating over the sand to make it less irritating. That becomes a pearl."

"Yes, that's right," Doc Pez said. He turned to Benny. "Why don't you go get the biggest shell over on that ledge? It's the tan one that has a spiral shape."

Benny took the shell off the shelf and carried it

very carefully over to the table. When he set it down, they could see the inside of the shell was bright pink.

"It's pretty," Violet said.

"This is queen conch shell," Doc Pez explained. "A conch is a soft-bodied creature that both makes its shell and lives inside it. The ones that wash up on the beach don't have the creatures in them any longer, but they did at one time. When a conch is inside the shell, it walks along the bottom of the ocean, like you would imagine a turtle walking along with its shell."

Doc Pez touched his necklace. "These come from a conch shell instead of an oyster, but the process is the same. These are very rare, though, much more rare than pearls from oysters. This island has always had a lot of conch shells wash up on it."

"Is that why it's called Isla de la Reina?" Henry asked. "Island of the Queen?"

"I don't know," Doc Pez said. "It's possible, I suppose."

"What's this we hear about you trying to change

the name of the island?" Dr. Iris said. "Isla de la Lusca! I couldn't believe it when I heard it."

Doc Pez slapped his knee and laughed. "You heard about that? I made that story up a couple years back. I told a fellow at the store I go to near the harbor about those legendary sea creatures called luscas. That fellow is a big gossip, and I knew he'd spread the story around. I hoped it would keep away the tourists, but I'm afraid it has done just the opposite. I've only seen more people coming around."

"We noticed that too," said Henry. "We saw a tour that was all about the lusca."

Doc Pez sighed. "I just had to do something. It isn't just about having tourists around. It's about keeping the area a safe environment for sea creatures, like the manatees."

"We heard another story recently," said Jessie. "Word has been going around town that the bay has mermaids in it."

"Mermaids that bite!" Violet added.

"Is that one of your stories too?" Dr. Iris asked.

Doc Pez looked confused. "Biting mermaids?" He laughed. "That's a new one. I certainly didn't start that rumor. If anything, I try to keep my stories about mermaids quiet."

"I'm afraid if that rumor continues to spread, it will bring even more tourists," Dr. Iris said. "And that means more trash."

Now Doc Pez got upset. He stood up and stomped out of the kitchen. "I can't understand who could have started such a rumor," he grumbled.

"So much for his good mood," Eric said. "I'm going to head back to the boat. I can sleep there tonight."

Benny gave a giant yawn.

"We've all had a long day," Dr. Iris said. "How about you try to get some sleep? We'll get the hammocks up, and then Gina and I can help Antonio clean up."

It took quite a while to get out the hammocks and put them up. When they were all ready, Jessie helped Benny get into his.

"It's kind of strange to go to sleep in a hammock," he said.

"But it's nice to be outside," Jessie said, climbing into her own. "And it's really nice to be on an almost-deserted island."

"Yes," Henry said. "And I'm glad we found the missing professor. But we still don't know where the mermaid rumors started. Doc Pez certainly didn't start them. He wants to keep his mermaid story a secret."

"There's also the Jenny Haniver that Katharine's grandfather brought," said Violet. "Where did that come from?"

Jessie thought back to the skeleton artifact they'd seen on the dock. "Could that have been the same one that we saw at Tía Chela's?"

Henry shook his head. "Remember, they looked different. Even Gina said so."

Suddenly, Jessie sat up straight in her hammock.

"What is it?" Henry asked.

"I just remembered something," said Jessie. "Gina

didn't ever see the Jenny Haniver at the dock. She had gone onto the boat already. I remember calling for her and her not being in sight."

"That means she must have already seen it!" said Henry. "Do you think that was what she had in the box at the fish market the first night we arrived?"

"I don't know," Jessie said, unzipping her mosquito netting. "But I think she has some explaining to do."

They went back inside. The others had finished cleaning up and were sitting at the table. They looked surprised when the Alden children came in.

"Is something wrong?" Dr. Iris asked.

"Not exactly," Jessie said. "But I think we've solved one mystery. Gina, did you make the Jenny Haniver that Katharine's grandfather bought? You said it had a different tail from the one we saw at Tía Chela's. But you didn't see the one on the dock."

Dr. Iris and Doc Pez both looked at Gina. At first she looked upset, and then she started to cry. Gina turned to Doc Pez. "We were trying to raise money for you," she said. "Me and some of the other students thought if we made an artifact and sold it, it could help. We weren't going to keep the money. We just really want to help you keep the island the way it is—as a place to study the creatures of the sea."

"Oh dear," Dr. Iris said. She looked upset.

Doc Pez did not look mad. Instead, he gave a small chuckle. "Don't cry, Gina. That's quite brilliant; though I suppose it's not the best way to earn money. I know you meant well, but I suggest you not make any more." He continued, "I've been thinking. It's about time I turn this island over to the university. They can maintain it and study the ecology here. As long as they let the goats and chickens and me stay for as long as we like, I'd be happy to let some youngsters pick up the garbage."

Gina wiped her eyes. "That would be wonderful."

The children were happy the truth about the Jenny Hanivers had come out and that Doc Pez wouldn't be alone on the island anymore. Still, they had some questions about their mystery.

"What about the stories about the scary mermaids?" Violet asked. "Did you start those too?"

Gina looked at the floor. "I thought if I spread rumors about the area, it would keep people away." She turned to Doc Pez. "I didn't realize you had tried that once before, with the lusca, and that it had backfired. I guess I have a lot to learn."

"What about Tía Chela's map?" asked Henry, thinking back to the faded writing he'd seen. "She said you tried to convince her that Mermaid Cove didn't exist."

"And when we got here, you pretended you didn't know about it," said Jessie.

Gina sighed. "Yes, it's such a special place. I guess I had the good sense to know that people would want to visit a place called Mermaid Cove, so I tried to keep it a secret. The secret's out now."

Dr. Iris gave Gina a gentle smile. "The good thing about stories is that just as easily as they come to life and spread, if no one keeps them going, they can disappear. We won't tell anyone about Mermaid Cove."

"And you could ask a journalist to put an article in the paper about the Jenny Hanivers, explaining that they are fakes," said Jessie.

"That's a good idea," said Dr. Iris. "I'm sure my aunt knows some journalists. Gina, would you be willing to tell someone how you made the Jenny Haniver?"

Gina nodded. "If you think it would help."

Benny yawned again.

"Well, this has been quite a day," Dr. Iris said. "I think it's time for everyone to get some sleep, unless there are any more mysteries left to solve."

The children started back to their hammocks. Violet was happy they'd figured out where the Jenny Haniver had come from and that they'd found the source of the scary stories about biting mermaids. She preferred to think of mermaids like the ones advertised on their kayak tour or like the one from Doc Pez's story. Violet wished they'd found some evidence that those stories were true. Suddenly, she stopped and turned around.

"There is one more thing," she said, looking at Doc Pez. "You said that the beads on your necklace—the mermaid pearls—came from conch shells. And that they are very rare."

Doc Pez nodded.

"But I am sure I saw one in the cave at Mermaid Cove. It was up out of the water, on a little ledge. How could it have gotten there unless someone put it there?"

Doc Pez smiled for the first time since the children had met him. "What I love most about the sea," he said, "is that no matter how much you know, it will still surprise you."

———

The next morning, it didn't take long for Eric to fix Doc Pez's boat, and they were soon ready to go.

"Good-bye. Don't come back," Doc Pez said, frowning at them. No one knew what to say, but then he broke out in laughter. "I'm just teasing. Come back any time. Just don't bring too many friends."

The boat ride back was very smooth, and the engine worked just fine. At the docks, they said good-bye to Eric. Then they spent the next couple days at Tía Chela's house, researching in the library and playing at the beach. As much as Benny liked learning about sea creatures, he was happy to be on dry land again.

"Well, I think we have plenty to cover for our episode on mermaids," said Dr. Iris, one afternoon.

"You aren't going to talk about Mermaid Cove, are you?" said Violet.

Dr. Iris shook her head. "I think we can tell the story without giving away everything."

"Is our adventure over?" asked Benny.

"I'm afraid so, but I have one more place to visit," Dr. Iris said. "You might say it's the beginning of our next adventure, and it begins tonight."

Everyone was so excited that they didn't mind packing their things, though it was hard to say good-bye to Tía Chela.

"I want to hear all about your travels," she told them as they got into the car. "Write me a letter."

"We will!" Jessie called as they drove away.

Dr. Iris brought them down a dirt road into a lush rain forest. Then she stopped, and everyone got out of the car.

"Are we camping in the forest?" said Benny. He sounded a little disappointed.

"Not in the forest," said Dr. Iris. "Above it! We're staying in a tree house hotel."

A woman emerged from a small building and brought them to where they were staying. Their room was a big tree house that looked out over a waterfall.

"This might be the most amazing place we've ever stayed in," Henry said.

"It is," Benny said, "but I thought it rained all the time in a rain forest."

"It does rain almost every day," Dr. Iris said. "A tropical forest is called a rain forest if it gets at least one hundred inches of rain a year."

Benny looked out again and then turned back to

them. He had a confused look on his face. "I think in this forest it rains frogs."

The others rushed out onto the balcony. "Look at this," Benny said, pointing at a tiny green frog sitting on the railing. "And then look out there and watch."

They watched until Violet cried, "I see one. There! It's falling out of that tree. And there's another one. Oh! They're going to be hurt when they hit the ground."

"But they're almost floating down," Jessie said. "Why are they jumping out of trees?"

"These are coqui frogs," said Dr. Iris. "They climb up to the forest canopy. But predators like tarantulas want to catch the frogs, so they climb up too. If a frog spots a predator, it will launch itself into the air to get away. The frogs are almost weightless, so they float to the forest floor and aren't hurt when they land."

She smiled. "There are many unusual plants and animals in rain forests. I thought it would give you a taste of our next adventure. We're off to a much bigger rain forest. Can you guess where?"

"I know Brazil has a big rain forest," Jessie said.

"You're exactly right. That's where we are headed, on an expedition into the Amazon rain forest."

"Wow," said Henry. "I've never heard of any legendary creatures that live in rain forests."

"You're going to be surprised by this one." Dr. Iris smiled again. "It's quite a creature, and I think we are going to have quite an adventure."

"I'm just glad this one will be on land!" said Benny.

Turn the page to a read a sneak preview of

MYTH OF THE
RAIN FOREST MONSTER

the final book in the all-new
Boxcar Children Creatures of Legend series!

"I don't see any rain forest." Benny Alden pressed his face against the car window. Outside, the streets were lined with buildings so tall that Benny could not see the tops. The only trees in sight were palms, growing along the sidewalk.

"We've still got a long way to go before we get to the rain forest," Henry said from the next row of the taxi van.

"That's right," said Dr. Iris. "Brazil is a very large country. São Paulo is almost as far away from where we are going as Greenfield is from Camp Quest, where we met. But this place is an important stop for our next investigation."

"It is? Are we looking for a creature that lives in the city?" Benny looked back out the window and searched for any sign of wildlife.

Over the summer, he had gotten used to keeping his eye out for unusual things. So far, the Aldens had looked for Bigfoot in the Rocky Mountains, elves in Iceland, and mermaids in Puerto Rico. Brazil was the last stop in the children's summer of travel. And

Benny was determined to find the best proof yet that the creature was real—whatever it was.

"You won't see it in the streets, I'm afraid," Dr. Iris said. "We're actually going to the zoo."

Benny's eyes got big. "The creature is at the zoo?"

"That wouldn't be much of a mystery, would it?" Henry chuckled and put down a map of the city. He had been helping Dr. Iris navigate, and he was the only other one who knew what they were going to see.

"I love zoos," said Violet. "But aren't we going to see lots of the animals in the rain forest, where they live?"

Dr. Iris nodded. "We will see many animals there," she said. "But it can be hard to spot animals in the Amazon. And there's one animal in particular that is good at hiding in plain sight. It just so happens to have some things in common with the creature we'll be looking for."

"Sounds like a sneaky animal," said Benny. He bounced in his seat with excitement.

Violet wrung her hands. Even though she was excited to be going to the rain forest, she also knew how wild it could be.

The taxi dropped off the children with Dr. Iris at the zoo. Once everyone had their tickets, the group walked inside. Immediately, they were surrounded by trees and vines and bright flowers.

"It's like stepping into a different world," said Jessie. Usually on the children's adventures, she was the planner. It was exciting for her not to know what they were going to do for a change.

Henry led them down a winding path through the zoo. Benny followed close behind, looking for a clue about what they were trying to find. They came to an enclosure of monkeys.

"Oh! Does the creature have really long arms and swing from the treetops?" Benny asked.

Dr. Iris shook her head. "We aren't here to see the monkeys."

Next, they passed an enclosure with a pair of yellow-and-blue birds.

"I know!" said Benny. "It's like a giant parrot with a big beak!"

One of the birds tilted its head from side to side.

Jessie laughed. "I don't think he liked you calling him a parrot, Benny." She pointed to the sign. "It says those are blue-and-yellow macaws."

"Oh." Benny turned to the enclosure. "Sorry, Mr. and Mrs. Macaw!"

"Just a little farther," said Henry.

He stopped at the end of the row and stood in front of the sign that said the name of the animal, so the others could not see. The enclosure had a grove of low-growing trees that shaded the whole area. Everyone gathered around and peered in. Even Jessie was excited to find what they were looking for.

Benny leaned on the railing. "I don't see anything in there. Are we looking for an invisible animal?"

Dr. Iris gave them a hint. "Look closely at the trees."

The children squinted as they scanned the treetops. Then Violet noticed something move among the leaves, and her eyes widened in surprise. "I see it!"

THE BOXCAR CHILDREN®

GREAT ADVENTURE

An Exciting 5-Book Miniseries

Henry, Jessie, Violet, and Benny Alden are on a secret mission that takes them around the world.

When Violet finds a turtle statue that nobody's seen before in an old trunk at home, the children are on the case. The clue turns out to be an invitation to the Reddimus Society, a secret guild dedicated to returning lost treasures to where they belong.

Now the Aldens must take the statue and six mysterious boxes across the country to deliver them safely—and keep them out of the hands of the Reddimus Society's enemies. It's just the beginning of the Boxcar Children's most amazing adventure yet.

JOURNEY ON A RUNAWAY TRAIN
Created by Gertrude Chandler Warner

HC 978-0-8075-0695-0
PB 978-0-8075-0696-7

THE CLUE IN THE PAPYRUS SCROLL
Created by Gertrude Chandler Warner

HC 978-0-8075-0698-1
PB 978-0-8075-0699-8

THE DETOUR OF THE ELEPHANTS
Created by Gertrude Chandler Warner

HC 978-0-8075-0684-4
PB 978-0-8075-0685-1

THE SHACKLETON SABOTAGE
Created by Gertrude Chandler Warner

HC 978-0-8075-0687-5
PB 978-0-8075-0688-2

THE KHIPU AND THE FINAL KEY
Created by Gertrude Chandler Warner

HC 978-0-8075-0681-3
PB 978-0-8075-0682-0

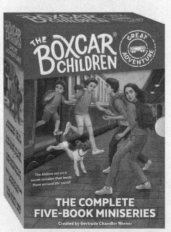

THE COMPLETE FIVE-BOOK MINISERIES
Created by Gertrude Chandler Warner

Also available as a boxed set
978-0-8075-0693-6 • $34.95

Check out The Boxcar Children® Interactive Mysteries!

Have you ever wanted to help the Aldens crack a case? Now you can with these interactive, choose-your-own-path-style mysteries.

978-0-8075-2850-1 · US $6.99

978-0-8075-2860-0 · US $6.99

978-0-8075-2862-4 · US $6.99

978-0-8075-2857-0 · US $6.99

Look out for
The Boxcar Children® DVDs!

The Boxcar Children and *Surprise Island* animated movie adaptations are both available on DVD, featuring Martin Sheen and J.K. Simmons.

Introducing The Boxcar Children®
Educational Augmented Reality App

Watch and listen to your favorite Alden characters as they spring from the pages to act out scenes, ask questions, and encourage a love of reading. The app works with any paperback or hardcover copy of *The Boxcar Children*, the first book in the series, printed after 1942.

Add to Your
Boxcar Children Collection
with New Books and Sets!

The first sixteen books are now available in
four individual boxed sets.

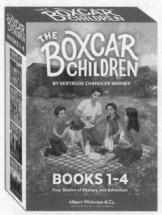

978-0-8075-0854-1 · US $24.99

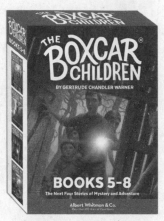

978-0-8075-0857-2 · US $24.99

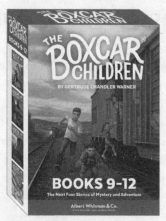

978-0-8075-0840-4 · US $24.99

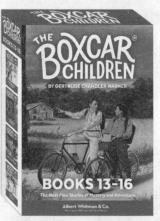

978-0-8075-0834-3 · US $24.99

The Boxcar Children,
Fully Illustrated

This fully illustrated edition celebrates Gertrude Chandler Warner's timeless story. Featuring all-new full-color artwork as well as an afterword about the author, the history of the book, and The Boxcar Children® legacy, this volume will be treasured by first-time readers and longtime fans alike.

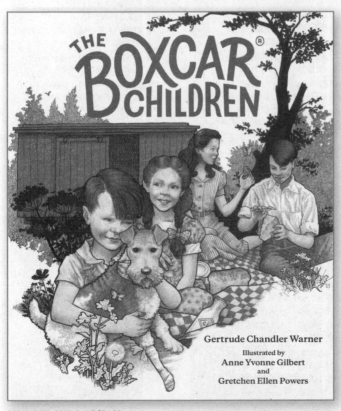

Gertrude Chandler Warner

Illustrated by
Anne Yvonne Gilbert
and
Gretchen Ellen Powers

978-0-8075-0925-8 · US $34.99

THE BOXCAR CHILDREN® MYSTERIES

GERTRUDE CHANDLER WARNER discovered when she was teaching that many readers who like an exciting story could find no books that were both easy and fun to read. She decided to try to meet this need, and her first book, *The Boxcar Children*, quickly proved she had succeeded.

Miss Warner drew on her own experiences to write the mystery. As a child she spent hours watching trains go by on the tracks opposite her family home. She often dreamed about what it would be like to set up housekeeping in a caboose or freight car—the situation the Alden children find themselves in.

While the mystery element is central to each of Miss Warner's books, she never thought of them as strictly juvenile mysteries. She liked to stress the Aldens' independence and resourcefulness and their solid New England devotion to using up and making do. The Aldens go about most of their adventures with as little adult supervision as possible—something else that delights young readers.

Miss Warner lived in Putnam, Connecticut, until her death in 1979. During her lifetime, she received hundreds of letters from girls and boys telling her how much they liked her books.